MW00948251

CLYDE the HiPPO

CLYDE GOES TO SCHOOL

by Keith Marantz

illustrated by Larissa Marantz

PENGUIN WORKSHOP

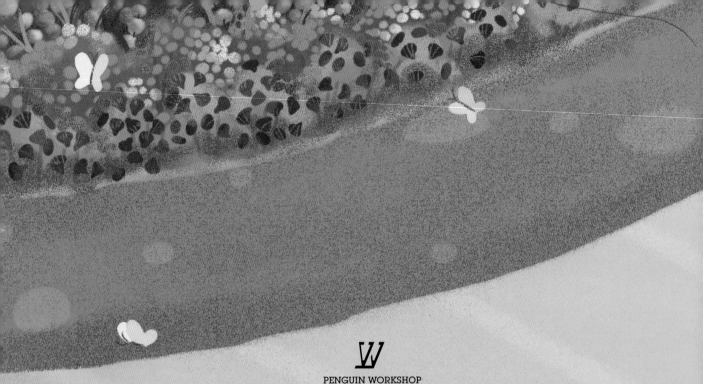

PENGUIN WORKSHOP
An Imprint of Penguin Random House LLC, New York

Penguin supports copyright. Copyright fuels creativity, encourages diverse voices, promotes free speech, and creates a vibrant culture. Thank you for buying an authorized edition of this book and for complying with copyright laws by not reproducing, scanning, or distributing any part of it in any form without permission. You are supporting writers and allowing Penguin to continue to publish books for every reader.

Text copyright © 2020 by Keith Marantz. Illustrations copyright © 2020 by Larissa Marantz. All rights reserved. Published by Penguin Workshop, an imprint of Penguin Random House LLC, New York. PENGUIN and PENGUIN WORKSHOP are trademarks of Penguin Books Ltd, and the W colophon is a registered trademark of Penguin Random House LLC. Manufactured in China.

Visit us online at www.penguinrandomhouse.com.

Library of Congress Cataloging-in-Publication Data is available upon request.

ISBN 9780593094457 (paperback)   10 9 8 7 6 5 4 3 2 1
ISBN 9780593094464 (hardcover)   10 9 8 7 6 5 4 3 2 1

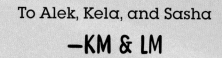

To Alek, Kela, and Sasha
—KM & LM

This is Clyde.

He's kind to everyone and everything. Even rocks.

Clyde spends his time

playing with his
chemistry set,

measuring furniture,

worrying,

and watching his favorite
TV show, *The Super Sloths*.

When he's outside, Clyde likes exploring his backyard with his trusty stuffed sidekick, Orson.

They especially love watching butterflies in the garden.

But Clyde won't have time to explore today.
Today is his first day of school.

Clyde wonders why his mother would do this to him since he already has so much fun at home.

"I think we should turn around," Clyde says when they reach the front gate. "Orson and I would like to go home."

"Clyde—you just have butterflies in your stomach," his mom replies.

"Butterflies? Mom! I would never eat butterflies. You know that!" Clyde says.

His mom smiles. "That's just an expression. It means you're nervous."

"Oh." Clyde scowls.

"You're going to have a great time," his mom says. "Just think of all the exciting things you'll get to do here."

Clyde shuts his eyes and tries to imagine what school will be like.

"You'll get to play games like hide-and-seek."

"You'll get to do puzzles."

"You'll even get to paint and do crafts."

"Then you'll get to have a snack."

Clyde opens his eyes. That doesn't sound like fun at all!

"I'm not going to school," he says. "I'm going home."

But as Clyde heads for the car, someone stops him in his tracks.

"Oh, hello—you must be Clyde," she says.

"I'm your teacher, Mrs. Mac. Do you think you can help me carry these butterflies inside?"

Clyde slowly nods—and grins.

When Clyde walks into the classroom, he sees paints and puzzles everywhere, just like his mom said.

But these look like *fun*! And his
neighbor Amanda is here, too!

He joins Amanda and a little giraffe at the coloring table. The giraffe is coloring a picture of the Super Sloths.

"That looks great!" says Clyde.

"Thank you," says the giraffe. "My name is Toby, and I love the Super Sloths!"

"I'm Clyde," says Clyde, "and I love the Super Sloths, too!"

"Well, Clyde," Toby says, handing him some crayons, "you're going to need turquoise and yellow for their capes. They were hard to find in the tub, but I'm all done with them now, so you can use them."

A dog named Dot joins them at the table. The four friends color until Mrs. Mac calls them over to the story rug. They're going to read a book about butterflies!

As Clyde races over to the rug, his mom calls out to him. "It looks like you're having fun, Clyde," she says. "Are you sure you still want to go home?"

"Actually, maybe I'll stay the whole time after all," Clyde says. "There are no more butterflies in my stomach. They're all in here!"

Clyde likes school!